baby radar

BY **Naomi Shihab Nye**

PICTURES BY **Nancy Carpenter**

Greenwillow Books
An Imprint of HarperCollinsPublishers

Baby Radar

Text copyright © 2003 by Naomi Shihab Nye

Illustrations copyright © 2003 by Nancy Carpenter

www.harperchildrens.com

Watercolor paints and a black pen were used to prepare the full-color art.
The text type is 24-point Highlander Medium.

Library of Congress Cataloging-in-Publication Data
Nye, Naomi Shihab.
Baby Radar / by Naomi Shihab Nye ; pictures by Nancy Carpenter.
p. cm.
"Greenwillow Books."
Summary: When her mother takes her out in her stroller,
a toddler encounters a variety of things, people, and animals.
ISBN 0-688-15948-6 (trade). ISBN 0-688-15949-4 (lib. bdg.)
[1. Toddlers—Fiction. 2. Neighborhood—Fiction.] I. Carpenter, Nancy, ill.
II. Title. PZ7.N976 Bab 2003 [E]—dc21 2002023165

1 2 3 4 5 6 7 8 9 10
First Edition

greenwillow books

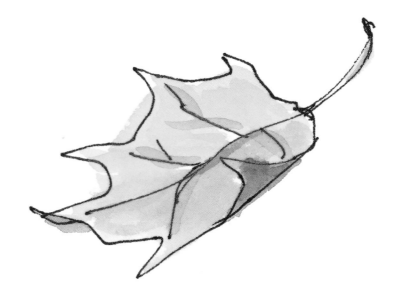

To Florrie, Clementine, Matilda,
and all stroller-riders
—n. ð. n.

For my radar-baby Maeve
—n. e.

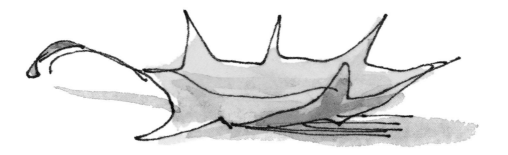

Out! Out!

Into the wind
on wheels

I love to see
the eyes of cars
their giant teeth
the red lights
on their behinds

Whoosh!

Fast!

Tires spinning

Truck tires close to the curb
Where do they go?

I'm going someplace too
up and down
the bumpity edge
stripey edge red edge

Tennis shoes daddy shoes sleepy slippers fat shoes
crazy shoes high-up heels fancy-dancy shiny shoes

I stretch my legs
to show my shoes

Ba-dump

Ba-dump

Mama meets people
Their knees bump my buggy

their shirts
in crispy bags
Sometimes
they lean over
say Cute!

I want to pinch
their noses

Hoo!
I want to untie their shoes

I see I see
big kids zip by
on wheels
Our neighbor Mrs. Marini
rides by
on wheels
She laughs when she sees me
We all have wheels

Giant trees
dropping leaves
in my lap
Spin them around
make them fly!

Throw them out
yellow on the ground
My wheels make
a crunchy sound

When smiley dogs pass
I reach for the fur
of the nice faces

Scrunch up
for the meanie mouths

Lost newspaper

stuck to a bench

Hot dog dropped

mooshy mess

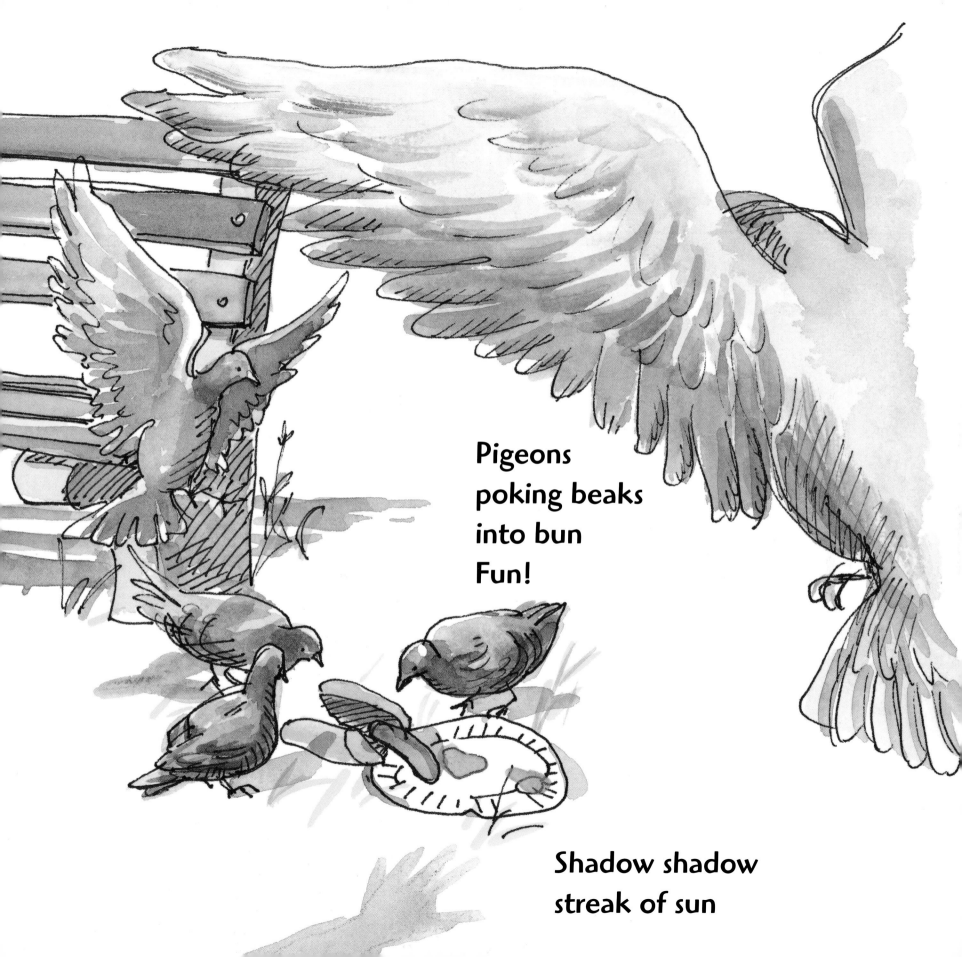

Pigeons
poking beaks
into bun
Fun!

Shadow shadow
streak of sun

A tissue from shopping bag

Wisssss!

I could catch it
in my fingers

Pull it

Out

Mama shouts
Not yours!

It's mine!

It's mine!

Everything's mine!

Roll fast

Mama unstraps my belt
I climb out
run behind
Mine

Mine!

My wheels pushing
Mama calls me
but I won't bump
a baby

Hey baby!

Hi baby!

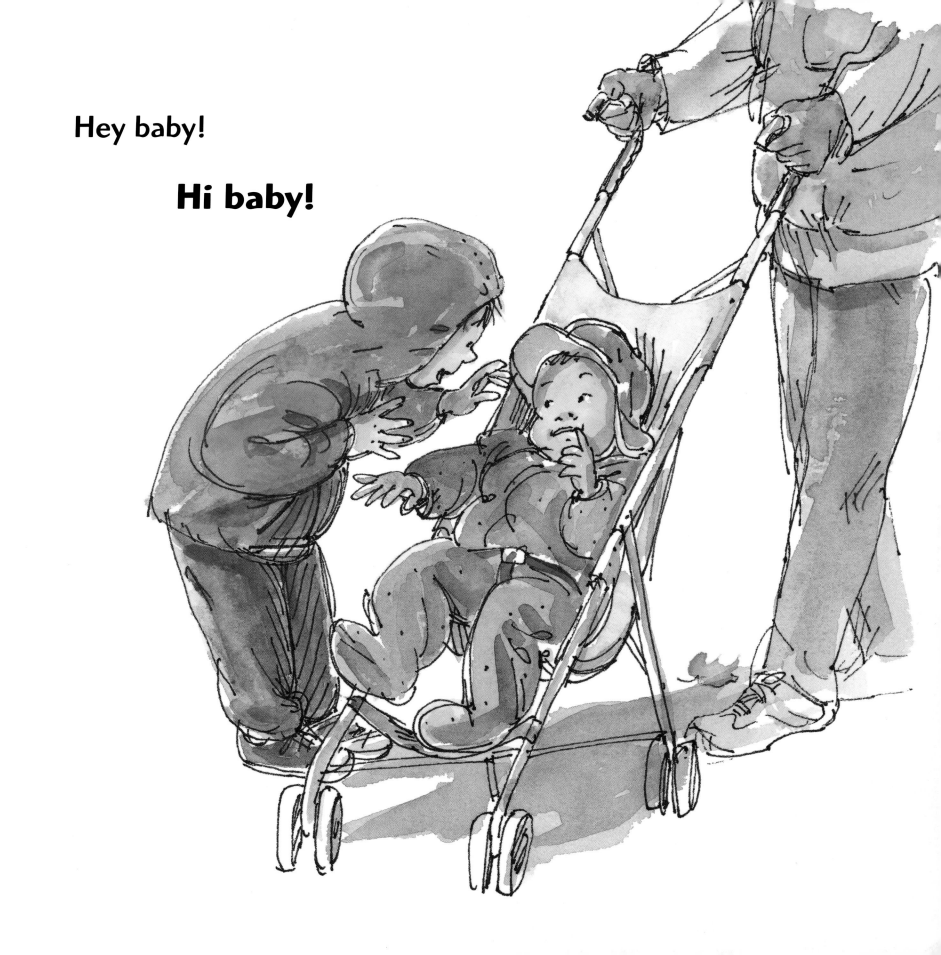

Mama chases
I am loose

Hello trash cans
Hello step

I climb
jump down
again
again

I will run
and run
and run
and

Stop

when Mama
catches me

Oh slow

Good grass
big stones
bread in a bag
feed the ducks

Ducks come swimming
dipping beaks

Ducks! Duckies!
Goose! Swan!

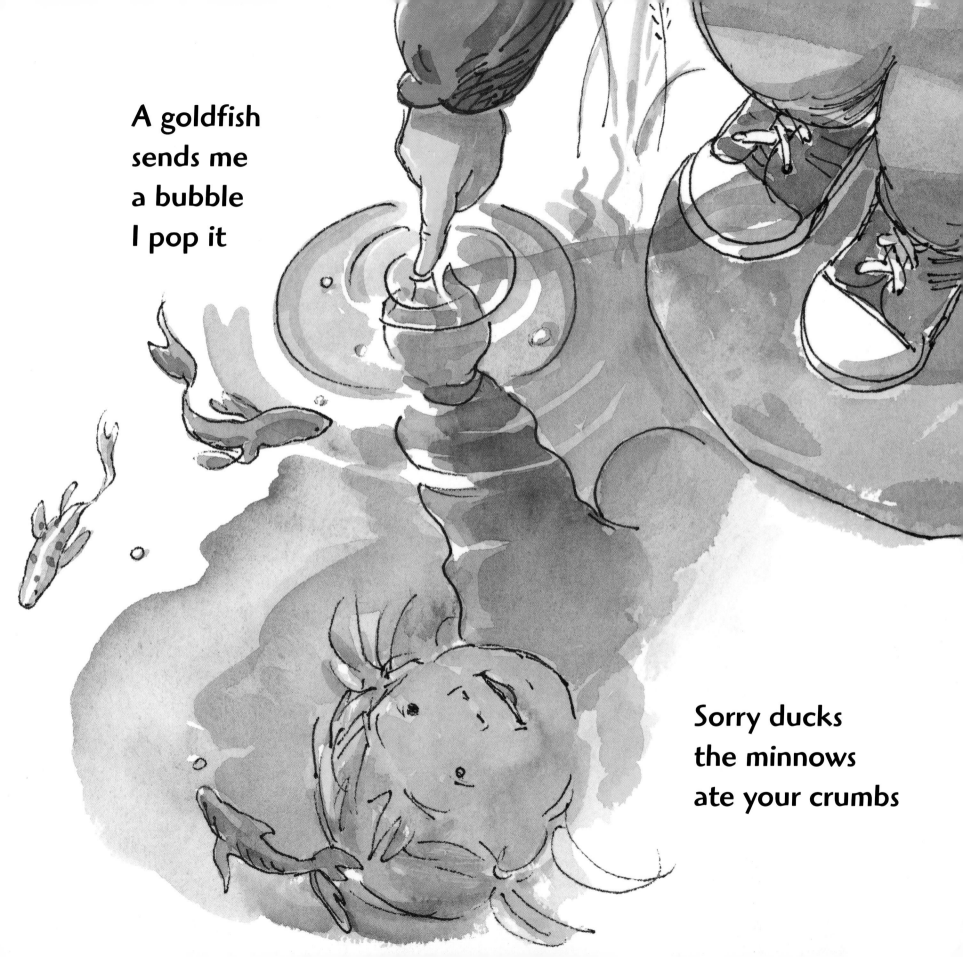

A goldfish
sends me
a bubble
I pop it

Sorry ducks
the minnows
ate your crumbs

I'm riding again
Tired

Where now?

In the window
a stroller going by

Sweeping

sweeping

man in apron
broom's
swishy
sound

Oranges

Sweet cookie wind

Mama loves

flowers

Two bunches

Stick my hand

into bucket

Wet

Sleepy skinny curly cat
turn around in circles cat
Blink at me cat

Kitty kitty

Wish I could take you

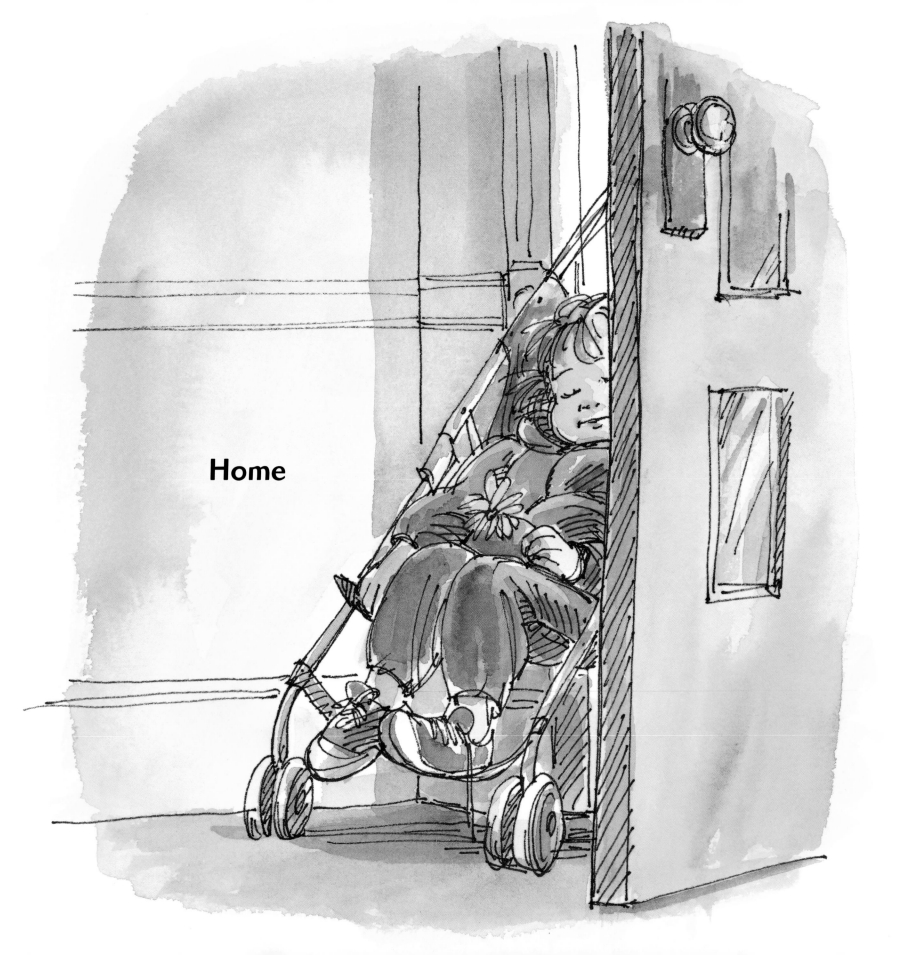

Home